The Viscount and the Minx

CHRISTINA DIANE

The Viscount and the Minx

Unlikely Betrothal Series

eBook ISBN: 978-1-964713-17-5

Paperback ISBN: 978-1-964713-16-8

Contents

Dedication

Dedicated to those who adore a protective husband who will also take you against a tree.

Note to Readers

Thank you so much for picking up my book—I'm truly delighted (and doing an undignified happy dance) that you're here!

Before we step into the historical world of Christina Diane, I wanted to share a little something about what to expect. While my books are set in the Regency era, I write with the modern reader in mind. You can expect stories that are character-driven, fast-paced, and heavy on the spice, with lively dialogue and plenty of heart.

I do my best to capture the setting and language of the time through research, but strict historical accuracy isn't my primary goal. Sometimes my characters insist on doing and speaking things their own way—and I let them. So, if you're looking for meticulous period detail and perfect historical precision, this book may not be what you are looking for (and that's completely okay!).

But if you're here for passionate heroines, swoonworthy gentlemen, witty banter, high stakes, high heat, and happily ever afters, all wrapped in a Regency-inspired world that welcomes diverse, bold, and intriguing characters—you're in the right place.

I hope this story sweeps you off your feet and carries you into a world of romance, tension, and a touch of scandal.

Much love and swoon,

Content Warnings

This book doesn't dive deep into the dark stuff—but you might encounter boundary-challenged relatives, oversharing friends, and a generous dash of spice. I aim to flag anything that might need a warning, but if I miss something, send me a message so I can update the list for future readers. To keep this message spoiler-free, you can check out identified content warnings here: https://christinadianebooks.com/content-warnings/

Chapter 1

Marina

Marina Villiers, Viscountess Ockham, drew a slow, measured breath as she lifted her pistol, the polished steel gleaming under the afternoon sun. Her grip was steady, her aim unwavering as she focused on the distant target nestled within the trees. A heartbeat passed. Then another. With a deliberate squeeze of her finger, the shot rang out, shattering the serenity of the clearing.

The acrid scent of gunpowder curled in the air as Evan, her husband, moved to inspect the target. Marina followed, her lips already curving into a victorious smile.

"Bull's-eye!" Marina exclaimed proudly. "I believe that means I have won."

"How do you do that?" Evan, Viscount Ockham, ran a hand through his raven-dark hair, shaking his head in amused disbelief. "It is positively unnatural how you never miss."

Marina surrendered the pistol to him with a knowing smirk. "I had an excellent tutor."

He examined the firearm before placing it back into its leather case. "The student has far surpassed the tutor."

Marina smirked at her far-too-handsome husband. "In more ways than one," she teased.

Evan scoffed, his grin flashing wicked and warm. "Hardly."

"Is that so?" She stepped closer, her voice dropping to a sultry murmur. The heat of the midday sun had nothing on the fire burning between them. And she loved needling her husband, especially when the outcome of such efforts was usually quite pleasurable.

His dark gaze smoldered as he reached for her, his touch possessive, fingers brushing the curve of her waist. "And just who was the one begging for more when I… broke my fast this morning?"

He wasn't incorrect. Marina's cheeks flushed with heat from the memory—her body arched beneath his, the sheets tangled around their limbs, his mouth doing wicked things that drove her senseless—sent a shiver down her spine.

"Perhaps I merely wished to boost your confidence," she countered, shifting to a whisper as she pressed against him. The scent of gunpowder mingled with his cologne consumed her, an intoxicating combination that made her pulse quicken.

Evan chuckled low in his throat. "Is that so? How remarkably generous of you, love."

Their eyes locked, and the air between them thickened. This place—the secluded clearing where he had first taught her to shoot—had always been theirs. From the first time she saw him, his thick black hair and mysterious dark eyes had entranced her. Their bond was a consuming force, an unbreakable magnetism pulling them together. And now, their special place was their sanctuary, the rest of the world melting away when they stood within those trees.

The wanton memories of their first meeting took over her as she stood before him, unfastening the buttons of his falls. "I'm known for my generosity."

"Known by whom?" His tone was tinged with a hint of something resembling jealousy. Even if they both knew there would never be another.

"Only you, love," she replied. Dropping to her knees in the grass, she took his cock in her hand and he sucked in a large breath of air.

"Such a perfect wife," Evan murmured in that low timbre that never failed to send heat coursing through Marina's veins.

She licked along the bottom of his shaft before sucking him completely into her mouth, reveling in the salty taste of his skin as she fell into a quick rhythm, bobbing her head on her husband's cock.

"Fuck," he moaned, threading his fingers through her hair, dislodging several pins. "I should lose to you more often."

Marina smiled around him as she worked her tongue along his shaft, shifting to a deliberate slowness, knowing it would drive her husband mad.

Evan's low groan echoed through the clearing, both hands gripping her head. She looked up at him, and their gazes met. Nothing but love and desire written all over his handsome face. "You're torturing me," he whispered, his voice strained as she swirled her tongue around him, her eyes not leaving his.

Marina pulled back and feigned a pout. "Am I?" she teased before kissing the head of his cock.

"Oh, you know exactly what you are doing," he growled, then reached down and picked her up as if she weighed nothing.

She wrapped her legs around her husband's waist as his lips came crashing down on hers, walking them to a nearby oak tree. He pressed her back against the rough bark of the trunk as their kissing remained intense and frenzied.

Marina moaned into his mouth as his hands worked at her skirts, bunching the fabric to give him access.

His fingers traced teasing patterns along her inner thigh, inching ever closer to where she ached for him. When his fingers brushed her pearl, she moaned into their kiss.

"Boosting my confidence?" Evan asked, kissing along her jaw.

His fingers circled her nub, applying the perfect amount of pressure, causing her to tighten her legs around her husband. "You have things well in hand."

"Do I now?" Evan drawled against her neck, his breath hot on her skin as he slipped two fingers inside her. "You're soaking my fingers, love."

Marina's eyes fluttered closed as pleasure coursed through her body. The contrast of textures—his smooth fingers, the coarse tree, the soft breeze caressing her flushed skin—heightened every sensation.

"I want you," she whispered, her voice catching as his thumb continued circling her pearl while his fingers curled inside her, teasing and tormenting.

The sunlight filtered through the leaves above them, casting golden patterns across Evan's face as he gazed at her with hunger in his eyes.

"Then come for me, love."

Evan gripped her bottom with one hand and increased the pressure and intensity with his thumb as he worked between her legs.

Marina's breath quickened as pleasure built within her, coiling tighter with each expert stroke of his fingers. She gripped his shoulders, nails digging into the fine fabric of his coat.

"Evan." She gasped, her head falling back against the rough bark.

"That's it," he murmured against her ear, his voice brimming with desire. "Let me feel you come undone."

When release finally claimed her, it crashed through her body like a wave breaking against the shore, powerful and all-consuming. She cried out his name, her body tightening around his fingers as he coaxed every last tremor from her.

He withdrew his hand and brought his fingers to his lips, sucking them into his mouth. His eyes burned with a mix of adoration and possessiveness. "Perfect," he murmured before capturing her mouth again in a kiss that left no room for doubt—he would always be hers, and she his. "Absolutely fucking perfect."

He gripped both of her hips and lifted her. "Guide me inside of you."

Marina, still breathless, did as her husband commanded, loving the way he filled her as he lowered her onto his shaft until she had taken all of him. Evan held her there for a moment, both of them trembling with desire, foreheads pressed together as they shared the same heated breath.

"You feel like heaven," he murmured against her lips, his voice strained with the effort of restraint.

Evan moved with slow, deliberate thrusts that made Marina's breath catch, lifting her slightly before letting her slide down his length again. Each movement sent ripples of renewed pleasure through her still-sensitive body. He never failed to turn her into nothing but a wanton puddle.

She gripped his shoulders, preparing for what her next command would do to her husband. "Harder," she moaned.

He turned feral, just as she knew he would. Thrusting into her as he pushed her flush against the tree. "See what you do to me?" he growled.

"Yes." She gasped, her fingers clutching him tighter, feeling the powerful muscles beneath his coat flex with each movement. It was the same reaction she had to him.

Evan groaned against her neck, his breath hot and ragged, and everything building within her released. She screamed his name as she came, tightening her legs so much she wasn't certain how he could still move. Then she felt his cock throb inside of her as he rested against her, pinning her to the tree while he whispered her name against her neck.

"You drive me to the brink of madness from how much I love you," he finally said, catching his breath.

"And what is it exactly that you believe you do to me?" she countered, her hand reaching up to brush the hair away from her husband's forehead. "Yet I love you, husband."

He placed a quick, tender kiss on her lips, then flashed her a grin. That grin made her heart catch every time, and he knew it. "In case you are keeping score, you might have won the little shooting match, but I believe I just won this battle of ours."

"Because I love you so much," she teased, "I shall allow you to believe that."

Evan gave her another quick kiss, then shook his head as he set her back down on her feet, helping her to right her skirts. "I suppose we should return."

"Would you mind checking in on Arthur?" Marina asked. "I want to see to my correspondence. I saw a bundle arrive this morning before you suggested our little contest."

Marina loved being a mother and loved her little family, but she also missed seeing some of her friends since they were missing the social events in London. Their son, Arthur, was still too small, and she didn't want to travel with him yet. And she didn't truly want to be apart from him for all the events, so her correspondence kept her connected to society until one of their friends might visit or perhaps next season.

"Of course, love. I'd love a bit of alone time with our son."

Evan was truly the best of husbands and the best of fathers. Her life couldn't be any more complete, and part of her felt a tad guilty that she also wished she could see some of her friends. Did that make her selfish? Perhaps, but she wanted it all.

Something caught her eye against the tree line. She stilled for a moment and hairs on the back of her neck stood on end. It felt far too familiar and brought back memories of when she had been taken by a horrible blackguard. She drew a deep breath as she took her husband's arm.

The man, whose name she refused to allow in her thoughts, was long gone and could never bother her again. Besides, even as she focused on the trees, there was nothing there. It was surely all in her head.

"Is everything all right, love?" he asked, clasping her hand on his arm with his free one. Evan's voice was steady, but she heard the edge of concern.

"Indeed," she replied. It wasn't a lie. Their life was perfect. She had a handsome husband who doted on her, who was the love of her life, and their adorable son.

Evan escorted them to their horses, and before Marina climbed into the saddle, she glanced over her shoulder one last time just to confirm for sure she had nothing to worry about. Thankfully, no one was there.

Chapter 2

Evan

Evan rocked in the nursery chair, his deep voice a soothing murmur as he read to his son. Arthur, barely four months old, had long since surrendered to sleep, his tiny chest rising and falling in a steady rhythm. Still, Evan continued, as he intended to for years to come. His own father had been distant and somewhat cold—a legacy he refused to pass on.

"… and the prince returned to his kingdom, having learned the value of honesty," he finished, his gaze lingering on the perfect bow of his son's lips, the delicate flutter of dark lashes against plump cheeks.

Carefully, he set the book aside, shifting Arthur slightly in his arms. His thoughts drifted to Marina, to the shadow that had crossed her expression in the field. Their afternoon had been… delightful. More than that, in fact. It was exhilarating, as it always was with her. His lips curved at the memory.

Since the doctor's clearance over a month ago, their physical relationship had rekindled with fervor. He could never get enough of his wife, and she had never been shy about wanting him just as fiercely.

Evan rose, cradling his son for a moment longer before laying him gently in the cradle. "Sleep well, little one," he whispered, lingering just long enough to marvel at the perfect miracle they had created. With a quiet knock on Nanny's door, he left Arthur in her care and slipped from the nursery.

As he navigated through the corridor, unease coiled in his chest. Marina had always been forthright, unafraid to voice her thoughts. An understatement, in truth. And yet, something had unsettled her—and worse, she didn't tell him. Was she truly content at Oxcrest? The doubt was absurd, unwelcome, yet impossible to ignore.

Descending the grand staircase, he forced himself to set the notion aside. And once he reached the study, he paused at the doorway, watching her.

Marina sat at their large shared oak desk, focused on penning a missive. Her quill moved swiftly across the parchment, her brow furrowed in concentration. She was stunning, no matter what she was doing. He would happily watch her at work for hours if he could.

She had redressed her chestnut hair after he'd mussed it earlier, and the sight of her graceful neck gave Evan a familiar tightening in his chest as he longed to kiss and mark her smooth alabaster skin.

His wife was breathtaking, and it still struck him in much the same way he felt the first time he'd seen her. But it was more than beauty that undid him—it was her mind, her fire, the way she looked at him as though he were the only man in existence.

And yet, something was troubling her.

Evan's jaw tightened. Whatever it was, she would not keep it from him for long. He wouldn't be able to stand it.

"Are you going to enter or is your plan to lurk in the doorway, my love?" Marina asked without looking up, a teasing smile playing on her lips.

Evan stepped inside, his gaze lingering on her as he made his way to her side. "Can I be blamed for admiring my wife? Perhaps it's your fault for being so damn tempting." He pressed a kiss to her temple, breathing in the soft, familiar scent of her.

She glanced up, love shining in her caramel eyes—and just like that, his breath was gone again.

"You already know, darling, that in any situation, the fault is always yours." She pointed her quill at him before winking, that wicked glint in her eyes making his blood run hot. The minx.

"Then by all means, love, punish me." He grazed his fingers across her collarbone, stopping just shy of the globe of her breast.

Desire flickered in her gaze, but she only smirked. "Later. Consider it part of your punishment."

"I'll hold you to that."

Her grin was pure mischief. "I shan't require a reminder."

Evan stole a quick kiss before settling into the chair across from her, picking up the day's paper. He told himself there was nothing to worry about. Marina had never been one for secrets. He was likely making something out of nothing in his head.

Evan read while Marina focused on her correspondence, settling into a comfortable silence.

"Juliana thinks she might be with child," she said after several minutes.

Evan lowered his paper. "That's wonderful news." His closest friend, Jude, had married Juliana recently—thanks to the meddling minx before him. Only a fool would doubt Marina's ability to orchestrate exactly what she wanted. And heaven help anyone who would oppose her.

She beamed. "But she hasn't told him yet—she wants the doctor to confirm first. So you mustn't say a word." Marina rifled through the letters. "Speaking of the devil, you have a missive from Jude."

Evan took the letter, broke the seal, and read. As he reached the end, a slow grin spread across his face.

Then he laughed. Too perfect.

Marina's brow lifted. "What is it?"

"Jude already suspects she's with child."

Marina stifled a laugh behind her hand. "Those two are hopeless."

"You aren't wrong," Evan said, setting the letter aside. "But you women underestimate how much we men actually notice."

"Do we now?" She scoffed. "And what, pray, have you observed?"

Evan studied her. There—just beneath her teasing tone, a flicker of something else. "You're keeping something from me."

Her eyes grew wide. "I… I…"

"Just tell me, Marina. You know you can tell me anything. Whatever troubled you back in the clearing—it wasn't nothing."

"Oh, that," she said quickly, glancing down at the desk. "I just wish we hadn't missed the season. That's all. So much happened without us."

She sounded sincere, but his instincts indicated otherwise. But he wouldn't press her further. At least not at that moment.

Evan reached for her hand, his thumb brushing over her knuckles. "There's always next year."

She nodded. "You're right."

"I usually am."

Marina scoffed. "Let's not get ahead of ourselves."

She opened her beautiful mouth to speak and then closed it again.

"What is it, love?" Perhaps he'd finally get to the heart of the matter.

"I thought perhaps we might host a house party soon. I was thinking about next month. What do you think?"

Evan's first instinct was caution. A house party meant disruption—especially for Arthur. "We just had Graham and Diana here, and we were in London for Hannah and Matt's wedding not that long ago. Perhaps a small gathering instead?"

Marina clasped his hand across the desk, eyes shining with excitement. "I want a grand event. After reading about all we missed in Town, wouldn't it be wonderful to have the house brimming with guests and festivities?" She caught his gaze. "Please."

They both knew he wouldn't deny her. He released a long sigh, resolved to his fate. "Next month, then?"

She nodded, slipping from her chair and making her way onto his lap. If he played his cards right, his 'punishment' might come sooner rather than later. Pun very much intended.

"Nothing too extravagant," she said, running her fingers along his collar. "I'm thinking of a fortnight-long party with a selective list of guests."

"And who exactly do you have in mind?" he asked, his arms circling her waist.

She beamed at him. "All our friends, though I doubt everyone will attend. I thought we could decide on the list together."

"Hmmm," Evan murmured, his fingers tracing idle patterns along the silk of Marina's gown. "And I suppose this has nothing to do with the letter from Lady Eliza that arrived last week? The one that had you pacing the study for an hour."

Marina stiffened slightly, color rising in her cheeks—stoking his desire. Either from how prettily she blushed or her position on his lap. Either way, desire stirred.

"You noticed that?" she asked, shifting slightly, and further threatened his restraint.

"I notice everything about you," he whispered, brushing his lips against her ear. A satisfied smirk touched his mouth as she shivered. "Including when you're avoiding my question."

She sighed, resting her forehead against his. "I see so much of myself in Lady Eliza. She's angry. Bitter. Over what, I don't know, but… I feel like she needs someone."

Evan arched his brow. "You're angry and bitter?"

She sat back, rolling her eyes at him. "Not anymore. But when you were a dolt… Well, I needn't remind you of my ire."

A loose curl had slipped from behind her ear. He tucked it back into place, fingers lingering. "I recall your ire being… intriguing." His lips brushed her temple. "Remember that when you punish me later."

Marina shook her head at him, stifling her laughter. "Perhaps someone was just as idiotic as you were, which would explain Lady Eliza's disposition."

Realization washed over Evan. He should have known. "So you aim to invite Lady Eliza and a few select suitors hoping to make a match?"

"That's not the only reason for the party," she admitted, lips curving into a knowing smile. "But it may have inspired the idea. Besides, I miss the excitement of social events. And if we can help friends and acquaintances find love—true love, the kind we've found—shouldn't we do so?"

Evan traced lazy circles along her spine, his focus wavering between the conversation and the far more immediate pleasure of having her in his lap. He could just haul her upstairs, or better yet, push everything off their desk to the floor.

She must have sensed his distraction because she stared him down.

"Have you forgotten how your last matchmaking scheme turned out?"

"Jude and Juliana are blissfully happy," Marina protested, a triumphant smile playing at her lips. "And soon to announce a new babe, it would appear."

"After considerable drama," Evan reminded her teasingly. "But Lady Eliza is a different matter entirely. If the scandal sheets are to be believed, Lady Eliza has turned down half of London's bachelors."

Marina laughed and playfully swatted his shoulder. "You read the scandal sheets?"

"Of course. Who doesn't?"

She rolled her eyes at him again. "Well, I believe I have a good measure of what she might be looking for."

"Should we bet on that?"

Mischief twinkled in his wife's eyes. "Help me make the guest list and then I shall see about taking you up on your little bet."

She rose from his lap with a victorious grin. He might've been disappointed at the loss—if he weren't so damn enchanted by his wife. She had already given him everything he wanted in life. And everything he hadn't even realized he needed.

If a house party made her happy, then so be it.

Even if he had the nagging suspicion that there was more to it than she was letting on.

Chapter 3

Marina

Marina practically vibrated with excitement as she planned the house party. If all went well, it would be talked about for seasons to come. And if she managed to orchestrate a few grand matches along the way, all the better.

She'd requested tea so she and Evan could work at their desk, sorting through potential guests. The missive from Lady Eliza had sparked the idea, but after the tricks her mind played on her earlier in the clearing, she realized just how much she needed a distraction. Nightmares still plagued her occasionally—remnants of her traumatic experience. She refused to put herself or Evan through that again. A house bursting with guests, conversation, and scandal would keep her mind too occupied for fear to take hold.

If she told him her fears, Evan would understand, of course, but he'd also blame himself for ever leaving her side that day. Which she couldn't bear for him to do. He'd done nothing wrong. Convincing him of that, however, was another matter entirely.

For now, she was simply pleased he had agreed to help. It would be fun to indulge in a bit of matchmaking mischief together. But before planning any elaborate entertainment, they needed a guest list—one filled with the most intriguing, entertaining, and possibly advantageous individuals. Ones who might take advantage of a country house party to pursue a bit of scandal and passion. Nothing facilitated a good betrothal quite like a country house party rife with temptation.

Sitting across from Evan, she took up a fresh sheet of parchment. "Juliana mentioned in her letter that Lord Demming has been rather lonely. I liked him when we met at the wedding. Perhaps we should invite him?" A lonely gentleman surrounded by eligible ladies… a perfect addition.

Evan nodded. "And I'd like to invite Nick, Lord Craven. He's been brooding over a woman for far too long—not that he'll talk about it. I think it would do him some good to get back into society. If you're so determined to play matchmaker, he could use the help."

Marina's quill flew across the parchment. A heartbroken lord with a mystery woman? She would get the story out of him one way or another. "We will need to keep the numbers even. So we must make sure we have enough women, too."

"Lady Preston?" Evan suggested. "She'd enjoy this sort of event."

"Oh! I adore her. And she'll certainly find company at a house party." The young widow had taken to pursuing trysts and sworn off love. Another perfect addition to tempt the men in attendance.

Evan chuckled. "If your goal is betrothals, you're wasting your efforts. Lady Preston will never marry again."

"Never say never, my love." Marina smirked. The widow had loved her husband deeply, but that didn't mean love wouldn't strike twice.

"What about the Duke of St. Albans?" she mused, tapping the quill against her lips. "If I could convince him to attend, I'd be the envy of every hostess."

Evan snorted. "Not a chance. You'd have better luck holding him at gunpoint."

Marina felt something uneasy in her stomach as if perhaps her tea hadn't settled well. It differed from what she'd felt earlier in the clearing. Her hand shot to her stomach, and she swallowed hard, fighting to soothe herself.

Evan's sharp gaze flicked to her immediately. "Are you all right?"

"I'm fine." She forced a steady breath, brushing off the memories of her abduction. It was nothing. Just old fears resurfacing.

Evan didn't appear convinced—and frankly, neither was she—but she seized the moment to distract them both. "And I'll take that bet."

Her queasiness subsided. She could do this. By the evening, it would all be long forgotten, and she'd be deep into planning the party of the season.

He arched his brow. "Bet?"

"The Duke of St. Albans. I'll get him here." She took a bite of her biscuit, needing something in her stomach.

Evan shook his head, amusement tugging at his lips. "If anyone can do it, it's you, love. But he will not show."

"We shall see." Marina smirked, feeling more like herself. "I also think we should invite Lady Juliet. She and Lady Eliza are close friends, and I like her a great deal."

They carried on for a while longer, narrowing down the list of the most promising—and scandalous—guests. By the time they finished, Marina held up the parchment and scanned the names, not including those of their closest friends. Nine ladies. Ten gentlemen. A perfect recipe for intrigue, flirtation, and—if she had her way—a few unexpected matches.

"I need one more lady," Marina said, sighing. "Perhaps I'll see if one woman wishes to bring a friend."

"You do realize you're not matching up ten couples, love?" Evan chuckled.

"Of course not," she said, waving him off. "But four or five seem perfectly reasonable."

"Four or five? That's ambitious even for you," Evan said, rising from his chair and rounding the desk. His hands settled on her shoulders, his touch warm and grounding. "Though I must admit, watching you scheme is rather… enticing."

Marina tilted her head back to look up at him, her pulse quickening at the heat in his gaze. "Is it now?"

His thumbs traced small circles at the base of her neck, and she felt herself melting into his touch. "Indeed. Although everything you do is enticing." He pressed a kiss to her brow. "Though I still maintain that St. Albans won't attend."

"You clearly underestimate my powers of persuasion, love."

"Perhaps a demonstration is in order," Evan whispered, his breath warm against her ear.

Marina's lips curved into a smile as she set down her quill. "And here I thought you were due for a punishment." She turned in her chair, but the movement sent another wave of queasiness rolling through her.

Marina masked the sudden discomfort with a smile, but her fingers clutched the edge of the desk. And she silently hoped the nightmares wouldn't also return that night.

Thankfully, the sensation passed quickly, leaving behind faint memories that seemed to hover at the edges of her awareness.

Evan frowned, his hands sliding from her shoulders to cradle her face. "Are you certain you're well?"

She always felt safer when he was near, even if she had long proven she could defend herself.

His thumbs brushed against her cheekbones with such tenderness that Marina nearly broke. For a fleeting moment, she considered telling him the truth about her fears. But voicing it would make it real. And she refused to let the fear win. She would focus on playing the part of hostess and it would all pass.

"Perfectly well," she assured him, turning her face to press a kiss against his palm. "Just a bit fatigued from all this planning."

His frown deepened. "Perhaps we should postpone the house party. It's a considerable undertaking."

No. That was the opposite of what she needed. But she couldn't explain it to him.

"Don't be ridiculous," she said, rising to stand before him. "I'm merely tired from sitting too long. Besides, I've already set my heart on this."

Evan's eyes searched hers. And she wasn't certain what it was he was thinking, but his protective urges were on full display. "Very well," he conceded, his fingers trailing down her arm to capture her hand. "But promise me you'll rest if you need it. The last thing I want is for you to exhaust yourself."

"I promise." And she meant it—she wouldn't push herself to exhaustion. Just enough to quiet her thoughts.

"I think," she continued, distracting herself from her thoughts, "that what I require most at this moment is fresh air. Would you care to walk with me in the garden?"

Evan's gaze softened as he extended his arm. "Nothing could keep me from doing so."

For the next hour, they moved through the garden, speaking of plans for the house party and what events Marina would host for the fortnight they had guests. The pleasant stroll with her husband calmed her nerves, and her stomach settled.

As they ascended the terrace steps, Baxter, their butler, approached. "My lord, your estate manager is waiting in your study. He says it's urgent."

Evan turned to her, lifting her hand to his lips. "I'll see you at supper, love."

She smiled back at him, thoroughly enjoying the way his breeches clung to his muscular thighs. That man was her undoing.

Turning back to the garden, she rested her arms on the railing, inhaling the crisp air. Birds flitted between the branches of a nearby tree, the picture of serenity. Then—movement. Something darted behind a tree. Or at least she thought it did.

Marina stiffened.

Her gaze locked onto a distant oak tree, its trunk thick and gnarled. Nothing. And yet, her skin prickled with awareness. She didn't see anyone, but she couldn't shake the fear that someone was there.

She had almost convinced herself that her mind was playing tricks on her. Then she saw it—a hand.

Her stomach lurched violently. She barely had time to turn before she cast up her accounts into the bushes below. Nausea wasn't a symptom she usually had when the memories of the past plagued her, but this wasn't just a memory if someone watched her from the woods.

Shaking, she wiped her lips with her handkerchief and forced herself to look again. The hand was gone.

But it had been there. She would stake her life on it.

Marina's breath came shallow and fast. She forced herself to stand still, to watch, to wait. Nothing. No movement. No shadow shifting from behind the tree.

Her mind was playing tricks on her. It had to be. Right? At least that was what she preferred to believe. It was the only truth she was willing to accept.

If she told Evan, he would insist on canceling the party. He'd watch her like a hawk, and he'd have her guarded every minute of the day. No, she couldn't allow that.

This would be something to laugh about in a few days. It would prove to be nothing but her imagination. And then, maybe, she'd tell him then.

Chapter 4

Evan

Evan had no idea what could be so urgent that Browning, his estate manager, needed to speak with him at this hour. If it wasn't truly pressing, Browning would receive a firm reminder of proper business hours—so Evan could return to Marina.

Striding into his study, he found Browning standing rigid before the desk, twisting his hands together. Unease prickled along Evan's spine. He'd never seen the man rattled.

"Browning," Evan said, closing the door behind him.

"My lord." Browning exhaled, the tension easing only slightly at Evan's presence. "I hope I'm not interrupting."

Evan motioned to the chair. "Sit." They could dispense with the pleasantries until he knew what the man was about.

Browning obeyed, but his posture remained stiff. "I was riding the estate today," he began. "And I encountered something—someone—I did not expect."

Evan's gut tightened. "Go on."

"A man. Gave me a note for you. Insisted I deliver it straightaway." Browning hesitated. "There was something about him, my lord. Something… not good."

Evan's pulse quickened. "Where?" What could the man possibly want? And why not just deliver the missive directly to the house?

"The north meadow. He came out of nowhere. I've never seen him before."

Browning extended the note. Evan took it, unfolding the parchment with deliberate calm. He scanned the page.

You and your pretty little wife will pay for the trouble you've caused.

The words struck like a blow. His blood turned molten.

He dropped the missive, raking both hands through his hair before snatching it up again as if rereading it would change the words. Fuck. Holy fucking hell.

"My lord?" Browning called out to him as Evan fought to gain control over himself.

His heart raced, threatening to burst outside of his chest as his breathing quickened. Who had dared to threaten Marina? It would be the last thing they ever did.

Only one man had a reason. An arse not good enough to lick the mud from a horse's hoof. But that bastard was locked away, beyond reach. Had someone else taken up his vendetta?

"And you spoke to this man?" Evan asked, barely maintaining his temper.

Browning nodded. "He was evasive. Left me with only the note and vanished as quickly as he came."

Evan forced his voice to steady. The weight of the message settled within him like a stone in water. "Describe him."

"Rough-looking. The sort you'd find in the city, not on our land. Alone, as far as I could tell, but I can't be certain."

"Keep watch for him," Evan instructed, the authority in his tone thinly veiling his anxiety. "If he appears again, I must know at once. Take no risks. There is nothing more important than ensuring my wife and son remain safe."

Browning inclined his head, his usual steadiness returning. "Consider it done, my lord."

Evan exhaled slowly. It wasn't enough.

"And the men—tell them to be vigilant, but keep this quiet. I don't want word of this getting out until we better understand what we are dealing with."

"I'll see to it personally." Browning rose, pausing at the door. "We'll sort this out, my lord. I'm certain of it."

Evan wished he shared the man's certainty. But Browning hadn't read the note. Browning didn't have a wife and child to protect.

The door shut behind him, leaving Evan alone with the rush of blood in his ears and the pounding in his chest. His fists ached to find the bastard responsible—to end this threat before it could take root.

Before he could stop himself, Evan read the note again. He vowed, with the same fierce determination he had shown during their last ordeal, that this time he would not be taken by surprise. This time, he would protect them all. No matter the cost.

He reached for the bell with the decisiveness of a man drowning, needing to ensure his family's safety.

A moment later, there was a knock. Baxter entered, his tone carefully measured. "You rang, my lord?"

"Yes." Evan turned, his expression grim. "I want footmen at every entrance. Night and day. And men patrolling the grounds at all hours. Effective immediately."

Baxter's sharp gaze narrowed. "Is there cause for con-cern?"

Evan hesitated. He trusted Baxter, but the fewer who knew, the better.

"A precaution," he said, his voice clipped. "And her ladyship shall know nothing about this."

Baxter nodded. "Understood, my lord. Anything else?"

A name. The name of the man who dared threaten his wife. Evan would trade his entire fortune for that single piece of information.

"Inform me immediately if you notice the slightest thing out of place."

"Is there anything specific I should look for?"

If only he knew. But any shift—any little change—could be the clue that led him to the bastard responsible. Damn whoever was doing this. "Anything out of the ordinary. Anyone who doesn't belong."

A vision of Marina being dragged from his arms struck like a physical blow. His grip tightened against the ache in his skull, a growl of frustration escaping before he could stop it. The study walls closed in around him, too small to contain the hellstorm brewing inside.

"I also want a footman stationed near the nursery at all times. And one shadowing my wife when she's not with me. Armed, but discreet." He met the butler's gaze, his meaning clear. "No risks."

"My lord, might you tell me what is going on?" Baxter hesitated. "I trust your judgment, my lord, but feel I may be better equipped to help if I understand what is happening."

Evan exhaled sharply, staring back at the man who'd served his family since he was a boy. "Someone is threatening my wife. It is the responsibility of this household to keep her safe. And unaware." His voice hardened. "I won't have her frightened."

It would break his heart for her nightmares to return. For her to thrash and cry in her sleep.

Baxter's expression darkened. "Are you certain it's wise to keep this from her?"

"You must trust me on this. She's suffered enough. I won't let this haunt her as well."

A long pause. Then Baxter nodded. "Very well, my lord. I'll need to hire additional men, but in the meantime, we can pull from the stables."

"Do whatever is necessary." Hell, he'd line up every man in Norfolk to link arms and form a circle around the house if it meant keeping Marina safe.

Baxter inclined his head. "I'll inform you once all is in place." He turned toward the door but paused, studying Evan. "We'll handle this, my lord."

Evan merely nodded, barely seeing him go. The worst scenarios played in an endless loop in his mind. If he closed his eyes, he'd be driven mad from the torture of it all.

He moved to the window, staring out over the estate bathed in the deceptive serenity of the pink-and-purple sunset. Someone was out there. Maybe watching. Maybe waiting. And there wasn't a damned thing he could do—yet.

His fingers dug into the window frame as he fought the rage within him at how helpless he was without more to go on.

"Darling?"

He hadn't even heard her enter.

Turning, he found Marina standing in the doorway.

"Come here, love." He opened his arms, exhaling as she melted against him. Her warmth, her vanilla scent—somehow, it steadied him.

She nuzzled against his neck. "Are you all right? Was something wrong with Browning?"

His mouth went dry. He hated lying to her. But her safety mattered more than the truth. Once the danger had passed, he'd beg for her forgiveness.

"Of course I'm well. You're here." He brushed a kiss against her hair. "And Browning is fine. We just need to hire a few more men to help with a few things."

"It won't prevent us from hosting the house party, will it?" She pulled back, searching his face. "I really want to do this, Evan. Please."

Dammit. The fucking house party. That was the last thing they needed. But if he refused her now, she'd demand answers. And Marina was too clever to be put off by anything short of catastrophe.

He would consider their situation flirting with the very thing, but unless he wished to tell her so. They were having a house party.

Unless… perhaps it was a blessing. If she kept herself occupied with planning the bloody event, she might not notice how frayed his nerves would be until the blackguard was identified.

He forced a smile. "Of course not, love. I'm sure you have the entire thing planned already."

Her eyes narrowed slightly, suspicion flickering there. Then, to his surprise, she let it go.

She pressed onto her toes, giving him a quick kiss. "It's going to be perfect."

"You shall be the hostess of the year," he murmured, watching her closely. She wasn't questioning him. That alone sparked suspicion.

Evan started to ask—but stopped himself. He was on edge. Seeing threats in every shadow.

"Supper should be ready soon," Marina said lightly, shifting the conversation.

"Then allow me to escort you," Evan replied, finally finding the grin he reserved for her. The one that always tempted his wife in ways that worked in his favor. "So we might see about that punishment of mine afterward."

He deserved far worse than whatever the playful punishment his wife had planned—for keeping this from her. But if it spared her even one nightmare, it was worth it.

Chapter 5

Marina

Marina wiped her mouth with a handkerchief, cursing her unsettled stomach. The nightmares hadn't returned, but the anxiety remained—gnawing at her, twisting her insides. Perhaps it was punishment for keeping secrets from Evan. For convincing herself she hadn't seen what she knew she had.

She'd spent countless hours at the window, watching the trees for movement, for some shadow slipping between them. Nothing. It would be easier to believe she'd imagined it—if not for the nagging unease that refused to leave.

And then there was Evan. He hadn't been himself since his meeting with Browning. When she'd asked, he'd brushed it off, assuring her it was handled. Which only confirmed that it wasn't. He should know by now he could talk to her, but no—he was a man about it. Bottling things up, letting pride and stubbornness keep him silent. She only allowed him to continue in such a manner because she kept her own secret.

With a sigh, she turned back to the desk, sorting through the growing pile of replies to her house party invitations. Almost all were acceptances thus far. Ironically, their closest friends had yet to respond. Hudson, Earl of Onslow, would attend—though not by choice. If anyone needed a wife to ease his perpetual brooding, it was him. Not that Marina held much hope of orchestrating a match. When it came to that difficult man, she would concede.

Lady Preston had requested to bring a friend, Lady Lily, which conveniently evened the numbers. That is, if no one declined at the last moment.

Movement at the door caught her eye. A footman. Again. She narrowed her gaze, and as if caught, he gave a stiff nod before retreating.

This was happening far too often.

When she'd questioned Baxter about the sudden increase in footmen, he'd claimed Evan had expanded the staff to accommodate the house party. A reasonable explanation. But she hardly needed to be babysat in her own home.

Then again… if someone was lurking in the woods, extra footmen weren't the worst idea.

She picked up another letter and immediately recognized the Duke of St. Albans' seal. Heart quickening, she broke it open. Scanning the contents, she let out an incredulous laugh.

"Well, holy hell."

"And what," a familiar voice drawled from the doorway, "has earned such a reaction from my perfect little minx?"

She smirked, not bothering to look up. "Lurking in doorways again? Some might call that stalking." The words left her lips before she could stop them. She glanced toward the window. Nothing there.

Evan strolled over and settled on the desk's edge. "Admiring, not stalking. There's a difference." He reached for her, his fingers trailing down her arm. "Besides, can't a man watch his beautiful wife at work?"

He never failed to make her heart flutter. And damn him, he knew it.

"Indeed, he may. But I wasn't aware watching me beat you in a wager was so captivating."

Evan pulled her to stand, positioning her between his legs. "Everything you do is captivating."

Leaning into him, Marina sighed as his arms encircled her. She fit against him perfectly, and his touch soothed her in a way nothing else could.

"Flatterer," she murmured. "You needn't try so hard. You've already won me, love."

He hummed, pressing a kiss to her temple. "Merely truthful. But do tell me—what wager have you bested me in? Because I do not admit defeat, except when you have a pistol in your hands."

Smirking, she grabbed the letter from the duke and handed it to him. "Read it and weep."

Evan's gaze flicked over the page. A slow, amused grin curled his lips. "I should know better than to underestimate my formidable wife."

She lifted a brow. "Perhaps one day you'll learn. Now, dear husband, what have I won?"

His hands slid down her backside, gripping the cheeks of her arse. "What do you want?"

"You already know."

Pleasure. Him. However he intended to deliver it—she had no doubt he would.

He lowered his lips to her ear, his voice molten. "Then be a good girl and lock the door."

Heat shot straight to her core. Without hesitation, she moved across the room and slid the lock into place.

When she turned, Evan crooked his finger, beckoning her.

Slinking toward him, she barely made it before he seized her hips, lifting her onto the desk. In one sweep of his arm, papers scattered to the floor. He urged her back, her head tilting over the desk's edge.

Cool air brushed her thighs as he pushed her skirts up, exposing her to him.

"If I had won," he murmured, his voice thick with promise, "I'd take your mouth just as you are positioned now." His fingers traced teasing circles along her thighs. "But since I concede victory…"

His tongue met her pearl, and she gasped. His grip tightened beneath her thighs, spreading her open further.

"Evan," she moaned. He knew her body too well. Knew exactly how to unravel her, leaving her panting and needy for her husband.

Marina's back arched, her head hanging further off the edge of the desk. Her fingers clawed at her skirts, desperate for something to clasp, holding them at her waist as his wicked tongue moved with agonizing slowness—from her pearl to her opening.

And then—lower. Much lower.

His tongue pressed against the forbidden place, sending a wicked pulse through her, making her pearl throb.

He knew exactly what he was doing. His fingers found her most sensitive spot, applying just the right pressure.

Three circles with his thumb pressed to her nub. That was all it took.

Pleasure radiated throughout every inch of her, scattering every thought. Stars burst behind her eyes as her body trembled beneath his touch. She shook from the intensity of her orgasm, allowing it to overtake her.

She barely had time to catch her breath before Evan pulled her upright, kissing her deeply. The taste of herself on his tongue only made her crave him more. And she was far from done taking her winnings.

"Sit in the chair," she commanded.

Evan smirked. "I'm bringing you with me."

She wrapped her arms around his neck. "That was implied."

Lifting her effortlessly, he stepped back and lowered them both into the high-backed chair. Her knees fit perfectly on either side of his thighs, and she wasted no time slipping her hand between them, unfastening his falls as she kissed and nipped along his throat.

"I thought I lost," he teased, tilting his head to grant her better access.

"And that is why you are under my control."

He let out a rough chuckle. "I'll remind you later who's truly in control." His breath hitched when she licked along his jaw.

Once freed, his cock stood thick and hard between them. Marina gripped the base, rose onto her knees, and guided him inside her as she sank down with a shuddering breath, fully seating herself.

"Fuck," he groaned.

"What was that about control?" She lifted her hips, then slammed back down, drawing another deep groan from him.

His fingers dug into her hips. "Have your fun, love. But we both know that by tonight, you'll be begging me to bend you over."

He wasn't wrong. She would. As much as she relished teasing him, she loved being at his mercy even more. And the bloody devil knew it.

Finding her rhythm, she rocked against him, shifting just right so he filled her perfectly. The pleasure built swiftly, but she cursed herself for not thinking to strip him first. His shirts and coat remained in the way, denying her the sight and feel of his muscular bare chest.

"Such a good little wife," he rasped, gripping her tighter, guiding her movements as he thrust up into her. "You ride my cock so well."

Marina leaned in, pressing her lips to his as he took over, his grip firm, controlling, driving her faster. She moaned into his mouth as her climax crept closer, fighting to hold on, to drag out the inevitable—

But she was lost. With one final thrust, pleasure shattered through her, sharp and consuming.

"That's it," he growled, holding her flush against him as his cock pulsed deep inside her, his heart racing against her from his own release. His breath came in ragged groans, his lips claiming hers in a possessive kiss.

Marina melted against him, her heart still racing. "I don't think I'll ever get enough of you," she whispered, her love for him thrumming through every inch of her.

He chuckled, tucking a loose curl behind her ear. "Good thing I had convinced you to marry me, then."

She rolled her eyes, swatting at his chest.

"There's my girl." He grinned and kissed her again.

As much as she wanted to stay tangled in his arms, she had things to do to prepare for their guests to arrive in a week. With a sigh, she rose from his lap, letting his softened length slip free before smoothing her skirts back into place.

"I must go to the village today," she said, pressing out the fabric. "I thought to take Arthur for some fresh air."

Evan, still tucking himself back into his breeches, froze. "What? Why?"

She frowned. His reaction caught her off guard. He'd never taken issue with her going out for a bit of shopping. "To get a few things for the party. And perhaps a sweet roll." She wouldn't deny herself the comfort of sugar after the stress of the past few weeks.

"Send someone," he said quickly. "You don't need to go for yourself."

Marina narrowed her eyes. What was the matter with him? "It's just the village, Evan. If you're so concerned, come with me."

His jaw tightened. "I don't think we should go at all when we can easily send someone in our place."

Something was off. Folding her arms, she tilted her head—both to study him and because she knew the way it shifted her breasts would serve as a distraction. "I am going. You can come or not."

"Marina—"

"Why, Evan?" she demanded. "Why is this an issue?" Could he know the secret she kept and wish to keep her hidden away at their estate?

Evan raked a hand down his face, glancing away. "There have been… robberies. It may not be safe."

She blinked. "In broad daylight? Evan, come with me if you're worried."

His exhale was long and slow, clearly displeased. "If we go, we're both carrying guns. And Arthur remains here."

She gaped at him. "Are you mad?" He must be. He'd lost his damned mind. Since when did simple village errands require an armory?

His gaze flickered down—finally noticing her breasts—and she knew he must truly be worried if it had taken him that long.

"I haven't gone mad," he said flatly. "But I won't take chances with your safety. Or Arthur's."

Marina sighed, stepping forward to cup his cheek. For all his overprotectiveness, she adored him for it. It was how he showed his love—for her, for their son. "If that is what you wish, I shall agree."

As she pulled him with her so they could ready themselves for the trip, a thought prickled at the edges of her mind.

Had she really seen someone in the woods, after all? Could it have been one of these robbers?

Perhaps she should tell Evan.

She shook off the thought. Not yet. Given his behavior, if she did, she doubted he'd let her step foot outside the house again. Not that he'd actually keep her from doing as she pleased, but it would certainly make their trip more pleasant if they weren't at odds.

But she would tell him when they returned. It could wait.

Chapter 6

Marina

Marina felt the tension in Evan's arm as she held on to him, his muscles coiled beneath her fingers. He hadn't been himself since they left the house, staring out the carriage window the entire ride as if expecting an ambush. If she didn't know better, she'd think he had seen something in the woods, too.

They retrieved her packages and sent them with a footman to load into the carriage. Evan barely spoke, his attention fixed on their surroundings, scanning every face, every shadow.

She looked up at him as they walked to see Evan scanning their surroundings, intently focused on each person they passed.

"The baker is just up ahead," she said, watching him.

"Mm-hmm," he murmured, gaze trailing a passing man.

"A sweet roll will be just the thing, don't you think?"

"Of course." His eyes didn't even flick to her.

He hadn't heard a word. She was sure of it. And she would prove it.

"An elephant would make a lovely pet, don't you think?" she mused. "We'll fashion a pen for it. I think I'll get one for Arthur." She smirked up at the sharp line of his jaw.

Evan patted her hand absently. "Absolutely. Anything you want, darling."

Marina stopped dead in the street.

He turned to her at last, chest rising and falling, eyes squinting as he searched her face. "What? What's wrong?"

She might have been touched by his immediate concern if it weren't so obvious something was going on. And she intended to find out what.

"I don't know. Is something wrong?"

Evan sighed, adjusting his hat against a gust of wind. "I don't understand. Is this some kind of riddle?"

Marina folded her arms, tapping her foot. She might kill him. "You just agreed to get our son an elephant."

"Children like toys. I'm sure we can have one carved," he said smoothly, far too confident for a man who had no idea what they were talking about.

Her irritation burned hotter. He would tell her what was going on if it was the last thing he did. "Something is wrong."

"With wooden toys?"

His attention wavered again, and his hand drifted to where his pistol was hidden as another man walked past. Marina glanced at the stranger—just a villager, minding his own business.

"That." She pointed. "That right there. You look like you're about to shoot someone for daring to exist."

"I do not." He waved her off.

"Evan." Her voice was steel. She yanked her hand from his arm, fists clenched at her sides. "Tell me what's going on." Each word was deliberate, heavy, meant to make him listen.

"Love—"

"No." She lifted a hand to silence him. "Something is wrong, and it's starting to scare me." She swallowed hard. Evan was her rock, her steady place. If he was on edge, then she had every reason to be, too.

"I told you already—there have been robberies."

He shifted on his feet. Lying.

"Don't lie to me. Please, Evan." Guilt curled in her gut. She had secrets, too—things she hadn't told him. But that didn't mean he got to keep them from her. At least that was what she'd continue to tell herself.

Evan glanced around, then cupped her cheek with one strong hand. She should pull away. Instead, she leaned into his touch, the warmth of him steadying her even as unease twisted inside her. Tears pricked at the corners of her eyes.

"All right, love." He sighed, closing his eyes for a long moment. When he opened them again, she saw the truth waiting there. And she knew—she wasn't going to like a word of it.

"Let's get your sweet roll," he murmured, pressing a kiss to her forehead. "Then I'll tell you everything."

Marina conceded, letting him lead her to the bakery, though she hardly believed she could eat the warm pastry he placed in her hands. Whatever he was about to say had already stolen her appetite.

After he paid, they departed the shop and settled on a bench beneath a large oak, watching the village go about its day. Evan tugged at his cravat, then ran a hand through his thick black hair.

"Love," he started, draping his arm over the back of the bench. "I only wish to protect you. Surely you know that."

"Protect me from what?" This was more than some phantom hand that might or might not have been there.

He hesitated. Then, "I received a note."

Marina's stomach twisted. "A note?"

If the man could just get to the point before her stomach became as unsettled as her thoughts.

"That's what Browning came to see me about that day."

She stiffened. She knew he had been off, but her victory could wait. "What did it say?"

Evan exhaled through his nose. "A threat. That we would pay for what we've done."

Her blood turned to ice. "What could we have possibly done?"

Evan's jaw tensed. "Can you think of no one who might have reason to hate us?"

Her breath caught. Of course she could.

She'd spent the last month convincing herself otherwise. That they had nothing more to fear. That the man awaiting the hangman's noose couldn't reach them.

But what if she had been wrong?

"How can we be certain?" she whispered.

"It's the only thing that makes sense, love. Until we know more, keeping you safe is all that matters. I can't lose you, Marina."

Evan's arm slipped from the back of the bench, pulling her close.

Her sweet roll tumbled from her hand, landing in the dirt. "I've been such a fool." She should have told him. What had she been thinking? By ignoring her instincts, she might have put them both in danger. And Arthur.

His brow furrowed. "What in the devil are you talking about?"

She swallowed hard. "I… I saw someone. Or thought I did." Marina wrung her hands in her skirts. "That day when we were—"

"Shooting," he finished, his voice sharp. "That's why you were acting so strangely. You saw someone. And you didn't think to tell me? Why on earth would you keep that from me?"

She shook her head. "I wasn't sure. I didn't actually see anyone, just… felt like someone was there. Then later, near the terrace, I thought I saw a hand—"

"Goddamn it," Evan growled, surging to his feet. "I would have sent every man in our employ to search the woods. How could you not tell me?"

"I didn't want to be afraid again, Evan. I didn't want the nightmares to return if I spoke my fears aloud. Truly, I thought my mind was playing tricks on me. And…" Her voice faltered.

"And?" His tone softened, but irritation still edged his words.

"And I didn't want to worry you. Every time I wake in the night, I see how it upsets you. I thought if I kept quiet, if I ignored it, the fear would fade." She let out a shaky breath. "But I've felt awful keeping this from you. My stomach has been in knots for days, making me dreadfully sick."

Evan ran both hands down his face, then drew in a deep breath. He reached for her, pulling her into his embrace.

There wasn't a single place in the world that felt as safe, or as right, as being in his arms.

His heart pounded against her ear, and he pressed a kiss to her temple. "My job is to protect you. Hang my feelings, love. If something threatens you, I must know."

She pulled back, meeting his gaze. "And it's my job to protect you. I thought I was—by keeping the nightmares at bay, by sparing you from the worry."

Evan's arms tightened around her. "Is there anything else? Anything you haven't told me?"

"No. I swear it. I'd almost convinced myself it was just my mind playing tricks." And now that it was out in the open, relief swept through her.

"You know everything as well," he said, his usual composure returning. "Let's retrieve the last of your packages and return home. The house party is in a week, and I'm no closer to putting a face to this threat."

It all made sense now—why he'd fought so hard against her coming to the village. She was suddenly grateful he'd been insistent about not bringing Arthur.

"I just need to stop at the dressmaker's. I ordered a few gowns for the party." The words felt ridiculous given the weight of their conversation. God, how she wished house party preparations were the only thing on her mind—that some faceless blackguard wasn't lurking in the shadows, waiting.

She patted the pistol in her reticule, finding comfort in its presence. Another thing she must thank Evan for.

"I shall try on the dresses at home and have her attend me there if alterations are required. But I agree that it's best we depart. I don't wish to remain in the village."

Evan gave her a pointed look. "You might recall I tried to dissuade this entire trip."

She rolled her eyes. So much for thanking him. "You had to say it, didn't you?"

He laughed, kissing her brow. "Just trying to lighten the mood."

Marina took his arm with an exaggerated huff, but he slipped his untouched sweet roll into her hand in a silent truce. Her heart squeezed. God, she loved him. Far too damn much. She took a bite, and they continued toward the dress shop.

Through the window, she spotted Mrs. Wilson arranging ribbons, alone in the store.

"Go fetch the carriage," she told Evan. "I'll be finished by the time you return."

His expression darkened. "No. I'm not leaving you alone."

"It's just Mrs. Wilson. You'll be gone for only a few minutes—and you have a clear view of the door."

He glanced around the street, jaw tight. "I don't like it."

She sighed. "We'll be home sooner if you just go. I won't step a single foot outside until you return."

A muscle ticked in his cheek. She knew he hated this. But when he sighed, she knew she'd won.

"Very well," he huffed. "But do not leave this shop." He kissed her quickly, then inclined his head toward the door.

Marina smiled and stepped inside, watching through the glass as Evan strode away. She laughed to herself at how quickly he took off once she was inside. He'd be back before she even had time to say a word to Mrs. Wilson.

"Lady Ockham," Mrs. Wilson greeted her with a warm smile. "Your gowns are ready. Would you like to come with me to the back and you can try them on?"

"Actually, if you could package them, I'll try them on at home. We're in a hurry to return to our son."

"Of course. Just a moment, and I'll have them ready for your footman." Mrs. Wilson bustled to the back, leaving Marina alone.

She idly browsed the ribbons, debating whether to add a few to her purchase—until a sound from the back room caught her ear. A muffled cry.

Marina stiffened. "Mrs. Wilson?"

No answer.

Her pulse kicked up as she called again, stepping toward the door. Just as she reached for the handle, a shadow loomed.

"Not so fast," a man sneered, leveling a pistol at her chest.

He was older—perhaps in his fifties—his gut straining against his waistcoat, his hooked nose casting a sharp silhouette under the brim of his low-slung hat. Though she couldn't see his eyes, the deep scowl twisting his face dripped with malice.

Marina's fingers twitched toward her reticule, but the man stepped closer, his gun never wavering. Sliding past her, he locked the door with an audible click.

"There we go. Can't have that idiot husband of yours spoiling the plan, can we?"

She forced her back to straighten. "What do you want?"

He laughed, a bitter, hollow sound. "Did you think you could send my cousin away and live happily ever after? With that meddlesome husband of yours? Raising your little urchin?"

Her breath came in quick beats, but she held his gaze, refusing to let him see her fear. She needed her pistol in her grip.

"What have you done with Mrs. Wilson?"

"She's alive. For now." He tilted his head mockingly. "But you? You're coming with me."

No. She couldn't let that happen. Not again.

"I won't."

"Fair enough," he said and lunged, grabbing her arm. "We'll see if you are content with your choice."

Marina wrenched back, fighting to free herself, but his grip was like iron. Just then, the rumble of wheels sounded outside—the carriage. Evan. He'd know something was wrong. He'd break in and this would all be over.

Before she could reach for her pistol, the brute shoved her backward into a dark space. The door slammed and the lock clicked into place.

"Let me out!" She pounded against the wood.

Laughter echoed from the other side. Then the footsteps retreated.

A rustling sound came from the darkness behind her. Marina reached out blindly and grasped a pair of trembling hands—bound hands. "Mrs. Wilson?"

She worked quickly, untying the knots. As soon as the woman was freed, soft sobs filled the space.

"He gagged me," Mrs. Wilson choked out. "Tied me up. What is he going to do to us?"

Marina swallowed, gripping her pistol inside her reticule. "I don't know," she admitted. But she wouldn't go down without a fight.

The door would open again. When it did, she'd be ready. She held her pistol out in front of her, ready to take her shot.

A pungent scent suddenly filled her nostrils. Smoke.

Her stomach twisted so hard, she almost fell to her knees.

"My lady," the man's voice called in a singsong lilt. "I hope you weren't expecting to see the light of day again. It's going to get a bit hot in there." A cruel chuckle followed. "Farewell."

"No!" Marina rushed to the door and pounded on it. "You can't leave us here!"

Hurried footsteps faded.

Panic clawed up her throat. Heat pressed in. Smoke thickened the air. Her lungs fought for breath.

Evan. Arthur. They would be left without her.

Think, Marina. Think.

How long did they have? Seconds? Minutes?

She coughed, forcing down the rising terror. *There's a way out. There has to be.*

Chapter 7

Evan

Evan gritted his teeth as his knee bounced relentlessly as the carriage slowed before the dress shop. He'd hated leaving Marina alone—he should have refused outright. From now on, she'd have no choice but to accept that he'd shadow her every step until this threat was over.

He leapt down and motioned for the footman to follow but froze when he reached the door. Locked.

Dread knifed through him. Evan pressed his face to the glass—and saw flames consuming fabric displays inside. No sign of Marina. Only a figure darting toward the back.

Fuck. Where was she?

"No!" he shouted, pulling on the door with all his strength.

"Get this door open!" he barked to the footman before sprinting toward the alley.

"Out of my way!" Evan shoved past a man in his path, barely slowing as panic drove him faster. He ran as if his life depended on it because it did. If something happened to Marina, and after he left her alone again against his better judgment, he couldn't go on.

Then—a gunshot.

His pulse thundered as he pushed his body harder, lungs burning, heart hammering like a drum. *Please, God. Let her be alive. Let her know I'm coming.* He would do whatever it took.

Rounding the corner, Evan spotted a stout man fleeing the building's back door—the bastard from the window. Evan didn't hesitate.

He lunged, tackling the man hard to the ground. They hit the cobbles with bone-jarring force, and Evan landed a savage punch. The man wriggled free just enough to strike back, his fist catching Evan's jaw. The pain barely registered. Evan grabbed the man by the throat, slammed him down, and drove his fist into his face—again and again—until his body went limp.

"Evan!"

Marina's scream broke through the haze.

"Thank God. Oh, thank you," he rasped, glancing back to see her. Relief surged so fiercely it nearly dropped him. "Get help!" he shouted. "I need something to tie this bastard."

The man barely stirred now, but Evan braced his knee on the scoundrel's chest, grinding hard as smoke thickened the air. The bastard had planned to burn Marina alive while Evan arrived too late to save her. And the thought sickened him.

"You'll never see daylight again," Evan snarled. "I will make sure of it."

The man coughed, blood seeping from his nose. "You'll pay… for what you did to my cousin."

Evan hit him again, harder. Hard enough that hopefully his bloody cousin felt it from prison. "You're the one who will pay. And soon your cousin will hang. You get to live just a bit longer since I shall turn you over to the magistrate instead of dealing with you myself."

By the time his footman arrived to help restrain the man, Evan had secured a gag around the man's filthy mouth. The least he could do was silence whatever poison he meant to spew.

Only when the villain was bound and secured did Evan rush to Marina. He grabbed her, crushing her against him.

"Please tell me you're unharmed," he demanded, his fingers skimming her arms, her waist—any sign of injury. His breathing wouldn't steady until he knew she hadn't been hurt.

"I-I'm all right," she said shakily, burrowing into his chest. "I was so afraid… I thought I'd never see you again."

He kissed her hair, her brow—anything to remind himself she was real. That she was and always would be his. "I'd have torn through those flames to reach you. You know that. But I heard a gunshot. What happened, love?"

She gripped his arms, grounding him with her touch. "I had no choice. He locked us in a closet and started the fire. I only had one shot, so I aimed at the lock—and it worked. Mrs. Wilson and I got out just in time."

"You're bloody brilliant," he said hoarsely, pulling her tight against him. "Have I told you that?"

"Not nearly enough," she teased weakly, her smile faltering. "Please… take me home."

"As soon as we speak with the magistrate." He cupped her face and brushed his thumb along her cheek. "I promise."

His lips claimed hers, heedless of their surroundings. He didn't care who saw—he'd been too close to losing her. Again. And he doubted he'd feel at ease for quite some time.

When the magistrate arrived, Evan gave his statement through gritted teeth, barely keeping himself from dragging Marina home on the spot. Only when the blackguard was hauled away in irons did some of the tension in his chest begin to ease.

"Let's get you home," Evan murmured against her temple.

"I love you," she whispered, her voice unsteady as unshed tears filled her beautiful caramel-colored eyes. His minx was a pillar of strength. She was the most capable woman he knew, and the only person she ever allowed to see her vulnerable side was him. And the sight almost broke him.

He swallowed hard, overwhelmed by the force of his emotions. "I love you too."

Marina leaned into him, her hand curling into his waistcoat. "I just want to forget today ever happened."

"You're going to let me take care of you," he said firmly. "Whatever you need."

"Please," she whispered, voice trembling as she submitted to his command.

The moment they were alone in the carriage, her breath hitched—a ragged, fragile sound that broke him all over again.

He hated that she'd endured even a moment of fear, and he questioned his choice to leave the bastard to the magistrate. But Marina needed him more than vengeance did. She was all that mattered—more than settling a score with a man whose fate was already sealed.

Evan held her tightly, stroking her hair, his lips brushing her temple. "You're safe now," he whispered. "I won't let anyone take you from me."

She curled into him, gripping his coat. "I know… I just—" Her voice faltered, and she shook her head, fighting her emotions.

"Tell me, love," he urged softly.

"I don't want to be afraid anymore," she whispered. "I can't face those nightmares again."

"You won't," he promised fiercely. "I won't let them. I'll spend every day showing you that you're safe. That you're loved. That you're unbreakable."

She let out a shaky laugh. "Spoken like a true knight in shining armor."

"Only for you." He sighed, tightening his hold on her. "We'll start with a long bath. I'll wash away every bit of fear you're still holding onto. You'll feel much better afterward."

She exhaled slowly, her body relaxing into his. "Perhaps you're right."

"I am going to remind you repeatedly that you just said that," he said with a hint of a smile.

Marina swatted his shoulder, the glimmer of her usual teasing returning. "Don't get used to it."

Epilogue

Marina

Marina was bent over the chamber pot, muffling her retching to avoid waking Evan. He'd worry—again—and he'd already spent the past week glued to her side. She wiped her mouth with a cloth, a small smile forming. The sickness had worsened since the incident at the dress shop, but this wasn't fear. She knew that now.

The nightmares hadn't returned, thanks to Evan. He'd kept her so relaxed, so loved, that fear hadn't dared creep back in. He'd doubled the footmen for added security, yet insisted life must carry on—and he'd been right. They couldn't live in constant dread.

But this… the nausea. It wasn't lingering anxiety.

When Juliana's letter arrived days ago informing Marina that the doctor confirmed her suspicions, the realization struck Marina like a thunderbolt. Of course. The exhaustion, the aversion to meat, the tenderness in her breasts—it was all familiar. And she couldn't believe she had missed it.

She wasn't sick with fear. It was so much more wonderful than that.

She was carrying their second child.

Marina rose to rinse her mouth and pressed her palm to her bare stomach, warmth spreading through her as a smile tugged at her lips. Another precious babe.

Strong arms circled her from behind, a familiar heat from bare skin pressing against her back.

"Might we celebrate together?" Evan's rich baritone rumbled low in her ear.

She leaned into him, grinning. "I don't know what you mean," she teased, though she doubted he'd missed the signs. He'd barely let her out of his sight for days.

His lips traced a path from her ear down her neck, the warmth of his mouth sending a delicious shiver through her. She was so in love with him, it bordered on obsession. But she supposed they were well matched in that regard.

"You haven't touched a bite of meat in days," he murmured, spinning her to face him. "I told you—you'd be surprised how much we men actually notice."

She looked up at him, her heart swelling. Of course he'd noticed. Her husband knew her better than anyone.

"We'll have the doctor confirm," she said softly, already confident she knew the truth. "After the house party."

He arched his brow. "This better be a damn memorable party, considering its timing. The whole thing is less than ideal."

"You doubt my abilities?" she challenged, lifting her chin.

His arms cinched around her waist, their bare bodies pressed flush. "I'd never doubt you in anything," he rasped, his hard length pressing insistently between them. "But if you think I won't keep fussing over you in front of a house full of people, you're mistaken."

She smirked, imagining the way they'd scandalize their guests—if they weren't too busy creating scandals of their own. And she would be lying if she said she didn't hope for that very thing. It would certainly make for a more interesting party.

"Right now," she whispered, her voice turning sultry, "all I want is you before our house fills with guests."

Evan swept her into his arms, grinning down at her. "You know I shan't deny you whatever you wish."

Marina wrapped her arms around his neck, kissing him deeply as he carried her back to their bed. Desire curled low in her belly, her body already aching for his touch.

The moment he set her down, she shifted to her hands and knees, glancing over her shoulder with a wicked smile.

"You little minx," he growled, massaging her backside. "Chest down."

She obeyed, lowering herself until her cheek pressed against the mattress. The air cooled her heated skin as his powerful hands spread her open.

Then his mouth found her.

His tongue traced her seam, slow and deliberate, sending fire through her veins. Her eyes fluttered closed, a moan slipping from her lips as he sucked her pearl with just the right amount of pressure.

"That feels so good." She gasped, rocking her hips back against his face. Pleasure coiled tightly inside her, and he didn't relent. When her release came, it shattered her—sharp, hot, and all-consuming. Overtaking her in intense waves for several seconds until it faded.

Evan ran his tongue along her seam again, tasting her as she trembled beneath him. "You taste incredible," he growled, sliding his tongue lower to tease her opening. "So wet and ready for me."

His hands gripped her hips, strong and certain. The head of his cock pressed at her entrance, his voice dark and rough. "Tell me what you want, love."

"You," she breathed. "All of you. Please."

He chuckled, low and dark. "It's not often my beautiful wife says please."

"Don't let it go to your head," she muttered breathlessly. Although she was feeling quite needy and edging ever closer toward being willing to beg.

Evan chuckled behind her. "That's my girl."

Evan entered her with agonizing slowness, torturing them both.

Marina's breath hitched as he filled her, stretching her with exquisite torment. Her fingers twisted in the bedsheets, her body straining for more. Impatient, she pushed back against him. She needed more.

"I love it when you're desperate for me," Evan rasped, pulling out almost completely before sliding back in with maddening control.

"Evan," she moaned, her mind too clouded with pleasure to form complete sentences.

His fingers dug into her hips, thumbs pressing into the dimples at her lower back. When he thrust again—deeper, harder—she almost forgot her own name. Her moans turned breathless, ragged, her body writhing beneath him as he set a punishing rhythm.

"That's it," he growled. "Let me hear you."

"Don't stop." She gasped, the pressure and intensity of her pleasure building so fiercely it robbed her of breath.

His grip tightened, fingers biting into her skin. One hand slid beneath her, his fingers finding her pearl and rubbing in tight, perfect circles.

"Oh God…" Her back arched violently. "Right there… Please…"

Unable to stop herself, she shattered, tightening around his length. Pleasure crashed through her in waves that left her quivering beneath him. Every inch of her body pulsed with bliss, her limbs trembling as if she'd never recover. And she wasn't certain she ever wanted to come down.

"Always such a good girl for me," Evan groaned, leaning forward to press his chest against her back. His cock pulsed inside her as he thrust in slow, shallow strokes.

His words made her wild and unhinged. She reached between her legs, covering his hand with her own and guiding his fingers over her swollen pearl. The heightened sensation pushed her over again, a softer climax, but no less sweet. She moaned low and broken, gripping the sheets for balance.

"And you," she breathed, "are so good for me."

No matter how many times they'd coupled, it was never enough, and it never would be. They collapsed together, skin slick with sweat, hearts pounding in rhythm.

Evan gathered her close, brushing her hair back from her face.

"I can't wait to see your belly swell with our babe," he whispered, pressing a tender kiss to her brow.

"Let's keep it our secret for now," Marina said, guiding his hand to her stomach. "It'll be fun to have this just for ourselves."

"You could cancel the house party altogether," he teased, "and I'll subject you to other titillating events for a fortnight instead."

She laughed, pushing at his chest. "The guests arrive today. We should dress—and spend some time with Arthur before the house is overrun."

Evan groaned theatrically, making her release a stream of giggles.

"The faster we're dressed, the sooner we can find an alcove in which we might scandalize the party," she teased.

"You should have led with that."

He leapt from the bed with impressive energy, and Marina couldn't resist watching the play of muscle across his back as he moved. She was quite a lucky woman, indeed.

Hours later…

The house was bustling with activity as carriages arrived and trunks were whisked away to the guestrooms. The staff moved efficiently, ensuring everything was well executed. Marina relaxed on Evan's arm, satisfied the party was off to a perfect start.

A footman passed carrying a small trunk. Evan's gaze lingered on the man, his eyes narrowing.

"What is it?" Marina asked.

Evan's focus shifted back to her, tension flickering across his features. "I thought he looked familiar."

"He's one of our footmen," she said lightly. "Of course he looks familiar." He was newer to the staff, but she had seen him at least once before.

"Yes… quite right." His smile returned, but it didn't reach his eyes. "I don't know what I was thinking."

Marina studied him for a moment, but the concern had faded. Whatever had unsettled him seemed forgotten. Still, unease prickled down her spine. All the bad things were behind them, right?

Of course they were, she told herself. The blackguards were all in prison.

Besides, they had the party of the season starting, and that required their full attention. And a date in the alcove with her handsome husband.

Want more Evan and Marina?

Get another spicy scene with Evan playing the part of an "edge lord" when you join my newsletter! And also determine if that footman was in fact someone familiar!

Join here for your free scene: https://dl.bookfunnel.com/fvozrnnfm0

Dearest Reader

Thank you for taking the time to read *The Viscount and the Minx*! I hope you enjoyed this spicy prequel read that introduces the concept for my Unlikely Betrothal series, where five different love stories are essentially taking place at the same time! Each book is a standalone with no cliffhangers, but the characters make appearances in each other's stories! I can't wait to introduce you to the other couples at the Ockhams' house party!

I am so thankful for all my readers and would appreciate it if you would leave an honest review on sites like Amazon, Goodreads, BookBub, etc.! Also, I'd love to stay in touch, so please visit christinadianebooks.com to join my mailing list and receive a free copy of *Only A Rake Will Do* (the Ockhams are in that one, too!), and stay informed on upcoming releases, promotions, and current projects.

If you are interested in being on my permanent ARC team and/or Street Team, send me a message on one of my socials! I'd love to chat!

I hope all of you will follow me and get the latest happenings and info on releases from my historical romance friends on any of my socials:

- Website: christinadianebooks.com

- Substack: @christinadianeauthor

- The Desire Den Discord

- Instagram: @christinadianeauthor

- Facebook: christinadiane

- TikTok: @christinadianeauthor

- YouTube: @ChristinaDianeAuthor

- BlueSky: @christinadiane.bsky.social

- Twitter: @CDianeAuthor

- GoodReads: <u>ChristinaDiane</u>

- Follow Me onBookBub: <u>Christina Diane</u>

- Join my Reader Group: <u>The Swoonworthy Scoundrels Society</u>

- Join my other Author Group: <u>Society of Smut & Scandal</u>

Hopefully I left you wanting more, so keep reading for a sneak peek at *The Earl and the Vixen* from the Unlikely Betrothal series! I can't wait for you to meet Nick and Eliza! You can also go ahead and get your copy of *The Earl and the Vixen* in paperback, ebook, and audio!

The Earl and the Vixen

"I love you, Eliza, and I intend to marry you. To hell with our fathers. Please tell me you want to be with me as much as I wish to be with you. In every way."

Elizabeth Nelson, the eldest daughter of the Earl of Nelson, melted into the arms of her sweetheart, Nicholas, who would one day become the Earl of Craven. She had loved him from the first time she'd come across him swimming in the stream that ran between their fathers' estates, almost five years ago.

Although the ownership of that very stream had been a long-disputed issue between their fathers. They each believed that the stream belonged to them and made trouble for each other when either household made use of it for livestock or to provide irrigation to crops. Ultimately, they both ended up using it for their estates anyway, and one would think they could be content with that. But a silly stream had been enough to cause such a rift that the men had sworn to hate each other. The bad blood only became worse between the pair over the years.

When she first saw Nick all those years ago, he hadn't given one whit about her back then. She had been far too young, and he had only been home for the summer from Eton, and by the time fall came again, he was gone. When he returned years later, he came across her reading a novel by the very same stream and finally noticed her, a woman and no longer an annoying young chit. They spent the next few months falling more in love each day and taking a few scandalous swims together at night in the stream in a rebellious slight against their fathers.

There wasn't a doubt in her mind that she wished to marry him, and she wanted nothing more than to give him every part of herself. To truly become his and make him hers. As a young woman of eight-and-ten whom no one spoke of such things to, she knew very little of what that would mean, but she knew she only wished to experience such things with Nick.

He would have offered to marry her already, and they would already be betrothed if they knew for certain how their fathers would react. Given the hatred the men harbored for each other, they feared that Eliza's father wouldn't agree to the union. With her age, they needed his approval to do so properly, or they would have to do something scandalous like elope to Gretna Green.

"I love you, too," she said, burying her face in his neck. "I want very much to be with you, Nick."

He took her mouth with his, kissing her with fervent intensity. When he broke the kiss, he brought her hands to his swollen lips. "Meet me at the hunting cabin tonight, after it is dark. We can be alone there, just the two of us with no one to disturb us."

She looked at their hands, attempting to mask her frown.

"What is it, Eliza? If you have doubts, we can wait," Nick said. He lifted her chin to meet his mesmerizing green eyes. His chestnut hair was just a bit longer than was fashionable, and it made him all the more roguish and handsome. "Look at me. I mean it, if this isn't something you wish to do—"

"It's not that," she said, cutting him off.

"Then is it something I have done? Did you not enjoy when I touched you…" his voice trailed off as he gestured towards her skirts.

"It is most certainly not that either," she said before swallowing hard. She had quite enjoyed it when he introduced her to the most exquisite pleasure she had ever experienced. "It's just that I know you have experienced these things before, and I haven't a clue what to expect or what to do."

Nick had always been honest with her, and he told her of his time at Cambridge and that there had been women who warmed his bed. He spared her the details, which she appreciated, but she wasn't so secure in herself that it didn't spark a flicker of jealousy, especially when she was about to lay herself bare before him.

She knew that the rules of society were different for men than women, especially since Nick was two-and-twenty and exposed to the things men do while at university, but it didn't mean she had to like it.

He cupped her cheek with his hand. "My love, you will be perfect. All I need is you. The rest we can explore together."

"But you—"

"Nothing that happened before you matters," he said, cutting her off, "and I know it isn't fair for me to say so, but I would be driven mad if I had to imagine even the mere notion of another man touching you. If I could change the past, I promise you, I would. Just know that

it is of little import to me. You are my future. My everything."

She pressed onto her toes and kissed him again. "I will
meet you tonight. I shall have to wait until after Papa goes
to bed if I hope to leave." Her papa would not approve of
her sneaking out to meet any man, let alone the son of the
Earl of Craven. He might have apoplexy if he knew she
intended to give Nick her virtue. Papa tolerated Nick's
presence when he came to call only because of the polite-
ness society expected. She was certain Papa would refuse
him if it wouldn't upset Eliza. Perhaps when she and Nick
married, their fathers might resolve things between them.
One could only hope.

He brought her hand to his lips again and kissed her
knuckles. "You had better return home before someone
comes looking for us," he said. "I will see you tonight, my
love."

She took his lips again for a few quick pecks and peeked
around the corner from the back of her family's stables,
ensuring no one could see her as she hurried back towards
the house. Her father might tolerate Nick visiting for tea,
but if he caught her with him unchaperoned, she wasn't
certain she'd see the light of day again. They had to get
creative to find ways to sneak off without her maid in
tow.

Eliza made it back to the terrace of her grand country home without anyone taking notice. As soon as she entered, she almost walked straight into her father.

"Where have you been, daughter?" he asked.

"I was just taking in the air in the garden, Papa," she lied. She didn't enjoy lying to her father, but she couldn't have him locking her away in her room. Surely love was a reason to justify the minor sin.

His brow furrowed, assessing her. "Where is your maid? You shouldn't be roaming the grounds alone."

"You are quite right, Papa. I just stepped out for a few moments after I was tired of reading. I will make sure Dot goes with me next time," she said, hoping her father wouldn't press her any further.

"Very well. See that you do. Did that boy call here today?"

"Nick?" she asked.

Her father nodded. "And shouldn't you refer to him as Lord Craven?" Hate spewed when her father spoke the title. "You aren't on familiar terms."

Eliza opted not to point out that her father should also refer to Nick by his title and not "that boy," but she opted to leave that unsaid. "Papa, he isn't his father and has done nothing to you. And no, he didn't," she replied. It wasn't exactly a lie since he didn't come calling to their door. "Perhaps he will come for tea tomorrow."

"You are to depart for town with your mama in a few weeks for the season. You are certain to marry before the season ends, so there isn't much point in the boy calling here, I should think," he said, his lips curled into a smirk.

"Perhaps he will offer for me and save you the expense of a season, Papa," she said, testing the waters for her father's reaction.

If she hoped to find a hint of his thoughts on her statement, she would be disappointed. His expression remained unchanged, other than a slight squint of his eyes.

"Perhaps," he said, "but you would have many acceptable options if you had a season."

She patted her father's arm. "The most important thing is that I marry someone who loves me, right, Papa?"

"And someone who is respectable and comes from an excellent family. Someone who would ensure you are provided for," her father said, his cool expression still unchanged.

"Of course, Papa," she replied. "I should like to return to the new book I just purchased with my pin money. May I be excused?" She wasn't ready to tell her father she had already made her choice and would marry Nick. Even if she had to run away with him to Gretna, he was the man she would marry, and there wasn't a thing her father could do about it.

"See you at dinner," her father said before departing towards his study.

Eliza continued to her room, unable to concentrate on reading as her heart wouldn't stop racing. She couldn't wait for her rendezvous with Nick later that evening, where she would learn what it meant to couple with the man she loved.

Around eleven o'clock, Eliza poked her head out of her room to see if anyone was lurking in the hallway. Dot had dressed her for bed a couple hours ago and set her hair into a long plait held in place with a ribbon before she sent the maid away for the evening. Eliza slipped on a serviceable day dress over her night rail and then covered herself with a pelisse to help keep from catching a chill in the cool night air.

Once she was certain there was no one moving about the house, she slipped out of her room and closed the door behind her. She made her way downstairs and snuck out via the door the servants used to access the kitchen garden.

The hunting cabin was only a ten-minute swift ride away, and she knew the route well. With a confident smile, she set off on the journey, assured of her safety under the luminous full moon. She crept to the mews, and a groom greeted her.

"Please saddle up my horse and tell no one that you saw me," she said, handing him a couple of coins.

He pocketed the coins and set off to do as she asked. Jimmy had done so for her a few times before, when she would sneak out to see Nick. The last time they snuck to the hunting cabin, she learnt what an orgasm was. Who knew that a man's hands could give such pleasure? She clenched her thighs together, already thinking about what delights he would introduce her to that evening.

A few moments later, Jimmy handed her the reins, positioning the horse by the mounting block. She thanked him and climbed into the saddle before flicking the reins and racing off into the night.

When she reached the cabin, Nick's horse was already tied up outside. He waited on the porch for her and came right beside her horse and lifted her down. "I'm so very glad you made it, my love. I would have preferred to escort you," Nick said, pulling her into an embrace for a quick kiss. "Let's get you inside. I already started a fire for us."

She grabbed his hand, and he led her inside. The warmth from the fire kissed her skin right away. She removed her pelisse and laid it across the back of the settee. She turned to face him, and in a single fluid movement, he swept her into his arms. Nick pressed his lips to hers, running his tongue along her bottom lip before her lips parted and he massaged her tongue with his. She returned his kiss, sucking his tongue into her mouth until he groaned.

He ambled her backward towards the bedchamber, not breaking their kiss, which grew wilder by the moment. Once inside the room, he kissed her jaw and neck, nibbling at her and then soothing the nips with his tongue.

Eliza sighed, loving the man before her more than she could have thought possible. She glanced around the room and noted he had started a fire in the bedchamber as well, and there were a few candles lit on the mantle above the fireplace.

Nick took her hands in his and leaned back to look at her. His expression was an intoxicating mixture of need and love, and with the light from fire casting shadows on his handsome face, it was an image depicted right out of one of her romance novels. His chestnut hair was almost black in the low lighting and the candlelight hit his green eyes just perfectly so that they shone like a precious gem. She lost her heart to him all over again.

"Are you certain you wish to do this?" he asked, placing a soft kiss on her jaw.

"More than anything," she replied. They had talked about waiting until they were married, but the desire to be with him had consumed her. She couldn't wait for her father to approve her choice. She needed to be with him in every way, and then they would fight for their future together.

A low growl escaped his lips, and he began working the buttons of her dress, unfastening enough that he could lift it over her head and then tossed it on the chair beside the bed.

Curious about what Nick would look like without his clothing, she unbuttoned the coat he wore and pushed it off his shoulders until it fell to the floor. She worked the buttons of his white shirt next. He remained still and allowed her to do as she wished, staring into her eyes as she undid each button and freed him from his shirt.

Her breath caught when she saw his muscular chest with a light smattering of dark hair. When she ran her hands across chiseled muscles and over his shoulders, he sucked in a breath, and the nerves she had about coupling with him evaporated, leaving only raw desire. She kissed his chest, becoming wanton and bold with each press of her lips to his skin. She used her tongue in the same way he did against her neck, and his muscles flexed beneath her touch.

"Eliza, that feels so good."

She licked and kissed his collarbone and up his neck, finding the lobe of his ear. She sucked it into her mouth.

He grabbed her head and kissed her lips again. After a few moments of exploration with their tongues, he broke the kiss and pulled her night rail over her head, leaving her naked before him.

She watched his response to her, and the hunger in his eyes only emboldened her further.

"You are so beautiful," he said, looking from her breasts and down her body. "I must taste you."

She wasn't sure what he meant, but he clasped her bottom and lifted her onto the bed. He tenderly laid her down across the massive bed and positioned himself on his knees between her legs.

He kissed her lips, then kissed his way to her breasts. Her entire body shivered from the sensation of his powerful form hovering over her and the anticipation of what he would do. She gasped when he took one of her nipples into his mouth and began suckling her. "Nick," she cried out.

"Do you like this?" he asked, stopping what he was doing.

"Oh, yes," she replied.

He dipped his head to continue, smiling against her breast every time she moaned or sucked in a breath.

When he used his hand to find her nub in the nest of curls between her legs, she moaned again.

He released her nipple and kissed his way down her stomach. He kissed lower and lower, shifting himself further down on the bed until his head was between her legs.

"What are you—" She cried out when his tongue flicked her pearl. "God, yes," she moaned.

He stopped and glanced up at her, a smirk playing on his lips. "Does that mean you wish for me to continue?"

"I may never wish for you to stop."

He gave a smug laugh and flicked her pearl again before circling it with his tongue. He inserted a finger into her core and moved it in and out. Her hands flew to his head, and she undulated against his mouth and hand.

She approached a release similar to the one he gave her a couple of nights ago with his hand, but this was different. Far more intense and wicked. When she tipped over the edge of her climax, she rocked and moaned, calling out his name.

He shifted himself on top of her and kissed her lips. She tasted herself on his tongue and licked the wetness off his lips. It was erotic and exhilarating, and she knew that once would never be enough.

"I could drink from you all day," he said.

"I may wish for you to do just that." She giggled when he laughed at her declaration. "I didn't know such a thing was possible," she said.

He kissed her again. "Would you like to stop now, or would you like for me to show you more?"

"I want more," she replied, the need evident in her tone. "Please, Nick."

Nick climbed off the bed and stood beside it, looking at her.

"Where are you going?" she asked, curving her lips in a playful pout.

"I must remove these now," he replied, working the buttons of his falls, his eyes not leaving hers. He pushed his breeches down to the floor and his member sprang to life, protruding from a nest of dark curls. Her gaze fixed on it, curious about what it might feel like in her hand.

He climbed back onto the bed and hovered over her, placing another sweet kiss on her lips.

"I want to touch you," she said, reaching between them to grasp the rod that stood erect between them.

He sucked in a large breath and closed his eyes when her hand closed around it. Balancing himself with one hand and his knees, he reached his free hand between them and wrapped it around hers. His cock was smooth to the touch but hard as steel.

"You can stroke me like this." He moved her hand with his, and she loved the power she felt from giving him pleasure the way he did for her.

She continued to stroke him for a few moments before he pulled her hand away. "I will spend if you should continue, and I would much rather do so after I make you come on my cock."

She bit her lip, enjoying his wicked words. "Tell me what you are going to do and don't be polite about it."

He slipped his hand between them and slid two fingers inside of her. "I'm going to replace my fingers with the head of my aching shaft, and then I'm going to move like this"—he slid his fingers in and out—"until you shatter and moan in my arms."

She released a sound that was a mixture of a sign and a moan. He pressed his lips to her ear. "Do you want me inside you now?" he whispered.

She nodded.

"Tell me you want me to make love to you with my needy cock," he said, kissing along her jaw.

"I want your cock, Nick," she whispered. "Make love to me. Now."

He withdrew his fingers and positioned himself at her opening. "This may hurt but not for long, and it shouldn't do so ever again."

He pushed himself into her with care, inch by inch. She gasped from the slight twinge of pain when he had his entire length inside of her.

"Are you all right?" he asked.

"Yes," she whispered, the pain subsiding, and she had the urge to move against him. "It doesn't hurt any longer."

He withdrew and then thrust back inside of her, causing her to see stars. She had never imagined such a pleasure and reveled in the intimacy from the man she loved most in the world filling her, the two of them joining as one. Nothing and no one else mattered but the two of them. He did it again, and she cried out.

"That's it, my love. Moan as loud as you wish. It drives me wild to hear you do so."

With every moan, he thrust deeper and harder inside of her. She wrapped her legs around him, and it became even more intense when he entered her as far as he could. He panted and groaned, and she pushed herself against him to meet his thrusts.

"You are mine," he said, thrusting hard and deep.

She responded with a loud moan and dug her fingers into his back.

"Say it," he whispered against her lips.

Eliza kissed him and broke the kiss to speak. "I am yours," she said. "I shall always be yours."

He thrust into her harder and faster.

"Oh, yes," she cried out. "Just like that. Don't stop." With each movement, she neared ever closer to madness and ecstasy. "Nick," she moaned.

He didn't relent and made good on his promise to make her shatter. When she did, she cried out his name again and bucked beneath him, arching her back. Once she rode every wave of the intense pleasure from her climax, he withdrew, his breath ragged. "God, Eliza," he groaned before warm liquid pooled on her stomach.

After a few moments, Nick climbed from the bed and removed a handkerchief from his pocket. He wiped between her legs, then her stomach, and set the handkerchief on the table beside the bed.

"I wiped away the blood, but you may be sore tomorrow. A warm bath should help," he said, settling in next to her and pulling her into his arms.

"That was more wonderful than I imagined," she said, brushing his hair away from his face. "I hope it was the same for you."

He pulled her tighter against him. "My love, I have never experienced anything as intense as being with you. I fear I am addicted to you and shall never get enough."

She giggled beside him. "Is that so?"

"It's perfect since you are mine," he said, kissing her forehead.

"Does that mean you shall meet me here tomorrow night and show me more?" she asked, placing a quick kiss on his chest.

"Nothing on this earth could keep me away."

Acknowledgments

There are so many incredible people—both new and longtime ride-or-dies—who have supported me on this wild writing journey. Authors, readers, friends, family, co-workers... you know who you are. I'd list every one of you if I had a few extra pages (and a really small font). Just know this: I adore you, and I'm endlessly grateful.

Steve: My husband, tech wizard, idea bouncer, chef, laundry hero, and all-around MVP. You believe in my big, bold dreams even when they sound like total chaos. Thank you for being my partner in every possible way. Love you, babe.

Dexter and Felix: My boys, my chaos gremlins, and the source of many laughs. You're excellent at distracting me mid-sentence, but you're also the inspiration behind some of the snarky sibling banter that sneaks into my books. One day you'll realize your mom writes smut... and I'll probably owe you both ice cream and therapy. Love you forever.

Rachel, Nina & Brittany: My mom, aunt, and sister—aka my built-in cheer squad. You've supported me through every high, low, and harebrained idea I've ever chased. You hold all my most embarrassing stories, so let's make sure you never talk to anyone without legal counsel present. I love you all dearly.

Erin: From the moment fate brought us together in the most unexpected way, we knew we were meant to be besties. Thank you for listening to every rant, dream, plot twist in life, and meltdown—and for always helping me find my way back to joy and clarity. You're pure magic.

Courtney: Fate handed me a twin flame in the author world. We literally finish each other's sentences (or just say the same thing) and have become legit besties. I can't wait for the day we meet in person. Thank you for our pretty much all day, every day chats, late-night idea storms, the pep talks, and all the chaos we've embraced together. We've got this, twinsie!

Morgan: The magic behind the scenes! You keep everything running, offer genius-level input, and somehow make it all feel easier and more fun. This book—and honestly, this business—wouldn't be the same without you. Thank you, thank you, thank you.

Bliss: Who knew a smutty follow train on Insta would bring me one of my dearest friendsies? Thank you for the endless texts, laughter, spicy scene brainstorming, feedback on my chaos, and all-around moral support. So lucky we found each other!

Rachel: You've read just about everything I've ever written, cheered me on, and gotten delightfully deep into this universe. Thank you for your thoughtful feedback and unwavering encouragement. So happy to have you on this journey.

To my **ARC and Street Team:** Your love, feedback, and support make my heart full. Thank you for shouting about these stories from the rooftops—you make this adventure feel like a party I never want to leave.

To **Dragonblade Publishing**: Thank you for believing in me and my words. I'm so excited to grow alongside such a passionate and supportive team, and be among your esteemed group of authors.

And to all the amazing **author friends** and **influencers** I've met through social media: You're one of the best, most unexpected blessings of this entire journey. Thank you for the inspiration, the laughs, the advice—and most of all, for welcoming me into this magical community.

About the Author

Christina Diane is an award-winning, bestselling author who loves to write super spicy, fast paced stories for the modern reader in the genres of historical romance and dark romance. Her historical romances are all set in the Regency era, with creative liberty taken within the historical setting to create a passionate, hot, intriguing story. Across all of her works, if you love combinations of high spice, witty banter, spirited heroines, forbidden romances, darker themes, and hot alpha men…then you are in for a treat! Because bad boys never go out of style!

She is a hybrid indie and traditionally published author with Dragonblade Publishing, Romance Cafe, and And

You Press. She reads mostly spicy Regency romances and all shades of dark romances, as well as thrillers.

Christina lives in Northern Maine with her husband and two boys. Her family also includes their three French bulldogs who go everywhere with them, as well as two solid black cats. The entire family is always up for new adventures. When she is not writing or chasing after her family, she usually has a Kindle in her hand!

Her writing journey began at the age of nine when she created her own comic strip, Grizzly Grouch. In adulthood, she was a freelance writer for several years, mostly writing lifestyle pieces for blogs. She found that she couldn't stop thinking about stories and characters, so much that she had to get them on the page! Christina frequently has dreams of random character ARCs that go into a massive list of planned writings. She currently has more than ten series just waiting to be written!

Aside from her family, writing, and books, she loves Bridgerton, the Grinch, Jessica Rabbit, horror movies, Chucky dolls, cold brew, yoga, Hamilton, the color pink, and speaking in obscure quotes from movies and TV shows.

Christina loves chatting with her readers and talking about great reads, so please contact her on socials! She'd love to hear what you think about her books and what you'd love to see more of!

www.ingramcontent.com/pod-product-compliance
Lightning Source LLC
Chambersburg PA
CBHW020733310726
48969CB00003B/812